KU-167-269

NICO

Recipes and recollections from one of
our most brilliant and controversial chefs

NICO LADENIS

PHOTOGRAPHS BY
MARTIN BRIGDALE

MACMILLAN

NICO

First published 1996 by Macmillan

an imprint of Macmillan Publishers Ltd
25 Eccleston Place, London SW1W 9NF
and Basingstoke

Associated companies throughout the world

ISBN 0 333 65177 4

The publishers would like to thank Thomas Goode
for the kind loan of crockery used in photography.

1 3 5 7 9 8 6 4 2

A CIP catalogue record for this book is available from
the British Library.

Photographic reproduction by Aylesbury Studios, Bromley, Kent

Designed by Macmillan General Books Design Department

Typeset by Florencetype Ltd, Stoodleigh, Devon
and Macmillan General Books Design Department

Printed and bound in Great Britain by BPC Hazell Books Ltd,
a member of the British Printing Company Ltd

I dedicate this book to Dinah-Jane, Natasha and Isabella,

who enjoyed living through our greatest success,

and to my dear friend, Bob Payton,

and much respected adviser, Sir David Napley,

both of whom narrowly missed being part of our celebrations

CONTENTS

ACKNOWLEDGEMENTS

When I published my first book, *My Gastronomy*, in 1987, I little suspected that the most momentous years of my life were in front of me. Nine years have passed since then and in that time my career has experienced the most extreme fluctuations. This book will, I hope, complete a circle round my twenty-five years of running restaurants. My achievements, disappointments and ups and downs have been fully shared, felt and lived by my family. It goes without saying, therefore, as many people know, that my life as a restaurateur and chef has been very closely bound with my wife Dinah-Jane and my daughters Natasha and Isabella. The elation and bitterness that we experienced along the way was felt equally by us all and the achievements were the result of a common effort. If my family has suffered in the process it is because we are inseparable one from the other, but the strength of our family bond ensured that the journey continued.

In any such years of endeavour, certain people and personalities always stand out. These people contributed much to our success. Some of the main characters are mentioned in greater detail in the book. I would like to thank some of the following for touching my career and for contributing a few bricks towards the final edifice: the late Neil Wates, Hilary Laidlow-Thompson, Geoffrey Weston, Clive Barda, Nico Kairis, Matthew Los, Richard Olney, Betsy and Johnny Apple, Annie and Henry Sweetbaum, Annette and Karl Ludvigsen, Sandra and Robert Clifton, Brian Calder, Patrick Collin, Alan Crompton-Batt, Yvonne McFarlane, David Wolfe, Mario Wynne-Jones, Hilary Rubinstein, Dr Zilkha, John Pryor and all the doctors who have kept us healthy.

I would also like to acknowledge the loyalty of those of our customers who have followed us with such patience through the many stages of our journey. This book is mainly my inspiration and that of my wife. The nitty-gritty, however, was due to the hard work of my chef, Paul Rhodes.

Finally, thanks to Martin Brigdale, who brilliantly photographed my food, Judith Hannam, my editor, and Mary Omond.

FOREWORD

I once tried to seduce Nico Ladenis' wife. Shortly afterwards I bombarded him with solicitors' letters threatening legal action. You could say that our relationship has not always been tranquil!

Before you get the wrong (or possibly the right!) impression, let me explain.

In 1960 I moved to a rather beautiful Victorian building, owned by my family, in Cornwall Gardens, South Kensington, London. The house was divided into a number of flats. I was on the first and on the top two floors was a very nice French lady, Madame Zissu. Madame Zissu had a pretty daughter. Her name was Dinah-Jane. I was twenty-five years old and made a bee-line for Dinah-Jane, inviting her downstairs to my impressive apartment, where I did my utterly feeble best to woo her with my charms. The event was a complete disaster. Nothing happened. But I remained on nodding, neighbourly terms with Dinah-Jane and her mother. Eventually Dinah-Jane acquired a real boyfriend. I would see him in the hallway and going up and down the stairs. We would exchange 'Good morning' or 'Good evening' according to what time of day it was. I remember Madame Zissu telling me her daughter's young man worked on the *Sunday Times* selling personal column advertisements.

After a while Dinah-Jane married the man in advertising. I never did know his name. They gave birth to their first child while still living above me in Cornwall Gardens. To my utter horror a pram then appeared in the narrow public hallway. I was extremely proud of my residence and the thought of visitors, when entering, having to dodge past a pram, appalled me. I was oblivious to the fact that it would be quite difficult for Dinah-Jane and her new husband, young and active as they were, to carry a pram up five flights of stairs.

I therefore bombarded them both, and Madame Zissu, with solicitors' letters threatening dire action unless they not only removed the pram but kept it from my sight for ever.

At the beginning of the 1970s I left Cornwall Gardens. Everyone in the building became a distant, and not much thought of, memory.

About four years ago I was taken, by a terribly important American music executive, to Chez Nico at Ninety Park Lane. Of course, I had heard of it. But I had never been there. I came in to the lobby and was extremely surprised when a middle-aged lady threw her arms round me and said 'Michael, we've been waiting so long for you to come!' I was totally bemused. 'Look!' the lady went on now with pride. 'There's Natasha!' She indicated a very beautiful girl sitting behind the Reception desk who also rose. We kissed gingerly on both cheeks. By now I was more confused. This was exaggerated by the arrival of a bearded gentleman in a chef's outfit. I recognized him from press photographs as Nico Ladenis.

'Michael!' he said, holding his arms outstretched. 'I can't believe it's you, I'm so thrilled, and delighted!' and he embraced me as a long lost friend.

These people are definitely mad! I thought to myself. I have no idea who they are. We have never met. It is all a terrible mistake. How will it end? The lady must have noticed this and said only two words: 'Cornwall Gardens.'

Suddenly it all came back. This was Dinah-Jane, the girl I had attempted to seduce some thirty years ago. There was Natasha, the child who had lain in the pram in my hallway, the one I had so desperately tried to have removed. And there was Nico Ladenis, the young man who worked for the *Sunday Times* in the advertising department, whom I had greeted on the stairs from time to time.

If ever there is a definition of the word coincidence, this was it.

Thus I was introduced to the cooking of Nico Ladenis. To say that I was impressed is an understatement. What I liked, and still do, about his food was the very delicate mixture of tastes and its basic simplicity. There is always a danger with chefs who have Michelin stars that they try to show off. Everything is just a bit too much. This is certainly not so with Nico. I have enjoyed every single course of every single meal I have had in his restaurant – and since that unusual first visit I've been back many times. My guests have always been very impressed and often surprised. I say surprised because Nico is one of the longer-running supercooks and to some degree the spotlight turns each year to shine on new people. It was by coincidence that I was in Nico's restaurant the night before he got his third Michelin star. I knew from talking to him he had long viewed that prospect as highly unlikely. He felt that other people were now in the limelight. I remember leaving the restaurant and saying to my companion, 'That food is really as good as anything you'll get anywhere in the world.'

So when I heard the next day that Nico had been awarded a third Michelin star, my first thought was that it was thoroughly deserved.

I know that when I go to Chez Nico at Ninety I will get a really excellent meal. The food aside, one of the other delights is to meet and be with such a wonderful family. They all have enormous charm, great natural wit, wonderful irreverence. They have given me much pleasure over the years and I know they will go on doing so in times to come.

Michael Winner

INTRODUCTION

Nico Ladenis has made an outstanding contribution to gastronomy in the United Kingdom and has had a colossal impact on the restaurant world. The oldest man, at sixty in January 1995, ever to be awarded the ultimate accolade of three Michelin stars, Nico has towered over the London restaurant scene since 1973, when he began his journey in Dulwich, a quiet suburban backwater of south-east London.

He was awarded a first star in 1981 and almost immediately a second at Battersea – another gastronomic desert – in 1984. In 1985, he ventured into suburbia to create a gastronomic temple on a grand scale. Despite the excellence of Chez Nico Shinfield, the good burghers of Reading were not ready for it. He returned swiftly and decisively to London.

Nico now presides over one of the world's greatest gastronomic destinations in London's Mayfair, having transformed the Grosvenor House, Ninety Park Lane restaurant into the ultimate Nico restaurant.

The two satellites – Simply Nico and Nico Central – were ground-breaking departures for a chef of Nico's quality, lifting bistro food to previously unheard of standards.

Nico has not courted controversy: it has been thrust upon him as a reward (or a price!) for an honesty and a focus that bewilder many journalists and commentators. His famous quote, 'The customer is not always right!' – a simple, frank statement – became entirely misunderstood by people who, presumably, believe that they are, in fact, always right about everything.

A major inspiration, even to those who would choose to follow a more orthodox path to success, he is always available to give help and advice to the many chefs who visit him, who eat at his restaurants and who write to him seeking answers to the inevitable problems of running a good restaurant in the 1990s. Nico is an example to all of them, especially the young men in the small towns of rural England, that excellence and patience can produce success. Many of them treat him as a father confessor and seek reassurance or encouragement after a bleak day's business.

When, in 1973, Nico opened his first restaurant in Dulwich, England was to embark on its voyage of discovery through the virtues and excesses of *la nouvelle cuisine*. Dinner was not a celebration of food but a social occasion, often a combination of both business and pleasure. Dulwich had no history of gastronomy and yet it was here that the intrepid Ladenis family, fresh from the ultimate tour of French restaurants, opened up shop for the first time. In an area chosen for obvious economic reasons, few have repeated the experience and none the success. Thirty-nine years old and self-taught, Nico was as firm of purpose then as he is now, perhaps even more so. He was certainly more volatile in those days and it is no surprise to learn that his reaction to his initial entry in the all-important *Good Food Guide* was to refuse to co-operate with the publication in year two because it failed to get its facts right.

Since he began work as a professional

chef, Nico has been at the heart of developments in the food world. Like everyone else, he, too, had developed over more than a decade, during which time good food and great chefs have become big news and the restaurant world has moved on to the front page of newspapers the world over.

Somehow, though, he is never a slave to fashion any more than he is to convention. The changes in Nico's menus come from his development and his ideas, not from public opinion. As the public began to scoff at large *nouvelle cuisine* plates on which chefs artfully presented mere mouthfuls of food, Nico took them, circled them in vegetables in a way never seen before in England, and gave them a new lease of life. However, the changes have always been carefully thought out and each dish is researched and practised. At a time when chefs are saying that they cook what they can buy at the market, Nico plans three months ahead. He knows exactly when the spring lamb, the wild mushrooms and the wild salmon will be available. He deals in quality not gimmicks. He demands consistency and loyalty from his suppliers, not party tricks.

Nico is, of course, a restaurateur, not just a chef. As fashions have changed, his dishes have developed. It is one thing to be a chef or even a good chef but to be a restaurateur you must understand one essential demand of every customer – whether a regular eater-out or an occasional visitor – and that is consistency. People do not have to be surprised every time they eat at Nico's restaurants and they know what to expect. His dishes do not change from day to day, nor do they change at the whim of a sous-chef who feels like slicing the meat a different way. Nico's menus and his wine lists have been short but well constructed since the beginning. The natural sense of balance, his good taste in eating that has been praised as often as his cooking, make him unable to understand why some people order a meal which is unbalanced or awkwardly chosen. To Nico, the whole experience of lunch or dinner has a shape and form and it is his job to help create that framework for the customer.

The achievement for Nico of establishing Chez Nico at Ninety Park Lane has been a family achievement. Isabella and Natasha were babes in arms on his first sortie to France to learn as a customer the high standards that could be achieved. Now they are two critical members of the management team at Chez Nico. Nico's wife, Dinah-Jane, was for many years his *Maître d'Hôtel.* Though no longer in the front line she is ever present in the background dealing with all the details and pressures of running the business in a calm and decisive way. Nico is one of the great chefs of this or any other generation. The fact that London now holds up its head in the world of gastronomy is due to Nico and the others who stood up for quality, standards, excellence and – at last – delivered the British public and London's visitors a restaurant culture they could value, enjoy and be proud of.

Alan Crompton-Batt

REMINISCING

I am sitting at my desk at Chez Nico at Ninety Park Lane. It is Friday, 20 January 1995. It's rather a grey day. The log fire is roaring in the background and I'm leafing through some cookery books. All is silence. I am contemplating the year ahead without enthusiasm or much excitement. Every Christmas our restaurants close for ten days. This year, quite exceptionally, Dinah-Jane and I had decided to take a few extra days in our new house in Provence.

My thoughts turned to our quiet corner of France, a tiny village called Callas. My mind focused on the silver grey-blue twinkling of our olive trees, the deep yellow of the mimosa in bloom, the crystal blue skies above us – all this reminded me of my idyllic childhood in East Africa. I had a wonderfully colourful childhood with inspiring parents. My father was an adventurer. He spent many years in America, came back to Greece to marry my mother, then settled in British East Africa. I was born in Tanganyika, went to school on the slopes of Mount Kilimanjaro and eventually went to live in the White Highlands of Kenya. East Africa in those days was everything a growing boy could want in life. Fast, flowing rivers from snow-capped mountains, dense forests, open plains full of game, semi-deserts with enormous baobab trees, spitting cobras and aggressive black mambas, a beautiful coastline with sandy white beaches, and much, much more. I fished for telapia on Lake Victoria and Lake Tanganyika. I hunted gazelle on the plains, blasted tasty green pigeons from fruit-laden trees and kept guard with a shotgun to stave off attacks on our chickens by agile hawks. In the wilds of Tanganyika, when the roar of the lions got too close to the house, my father let off his shotgun in the middle of the night to frighten them away.

My education thus far was colonial public school. But I was always ambitious and wanted to get to the top, so, at seventeen, I came to England to prepare for university. After three years in London, I went to Hull University to read Economics. Some contrast! In place of the jacarandas, oleanders and bougainvilleas, there was snow, snow, snow. I graduated at the age of twenty-four and spent the next thirteen years floundering in and out of large corporations, never fitting into the managerial structure, getting disillusioned and frustrated as I went along: the California Texas Oil Corporation, the Ford Motor Company, the Thomson Organization – all very prestigious companies, but not right for me. I was not fulfilled and kept on dreaming.

Then, at the *Sunday Times*, I met my wife, Dinah-Jane, a momentous event in my life. Together we developed a taste for good food and good wine. My wife's French background encouraged this new-found interest, so much so that we took a year's sabbatical and went to live with her relatives in Provence. There, the idea of opening a restaurant took seed. It wasn't to be just any restaurant. It had to be a very good restaurant with fantastic French food. It had to be the best in London. I finally came to grips with my dream, began to turn it into reality and inexorably, by sheer graft and

determination, propelled myself towards the top. Just as politicians strive for the cabinet posts and honours lists, and actors have their Oscars, in gastronomy I had but one goal. The ultimate prize for me was to have three Michelin stars.

The telephone is playing its usual January tune – dead silence! My mind starts to roam. I am sixty years old. I have been in this business for nearly twenty-five years. My daughters were very young when we began in Dulwich. My mind wanders to the beginning. I came from nowhere, I started with nothing. All I had was arrogance and a burning determination to succeed. I recalled how I spent one full year looking for premises in Kensington and Chelsea to begin my first venture. My funds were dwindling and I was becoming desperate. I had to cast my net wider, since, in the early 1970s, getting planning permission for a restaurant in those areas was nearly impossible. That is how we came to end up in Lordship Lane, East Dulwich. As it turned out, Dulwich was the ideal spot for us to begin. It was an important focus of the professional middle classes. The magnet was the college and the great teaching hospitals. This ensured a population of teachers, doctors, barristers, journalists, architects and artists. Although our premises were not located in Dulwich Village, our customers did not have to travel far. The eccentric nature of my character struck a chord with these people.

Chez Nico in Dulwich consumed all our capital, but the set-up costs were so low in comparison with today's prices that it proved a comfortable background for a dedicated amateur to learn his profession. Renovations and set-up costs were approximately £5,000, half of which was provided by an understanding bank manager, the rest by Colonel Aitken Lawrie, who turned out to be the perfect partner. He is a true English gentleman who has served his country all over the world and knows many languages. We liked each other instantly when we met at the time of the birth of our second daughter, Isabella. He always said he would help us – and he did. At the age of eighty-two he visits us regularly for a slap-up meal.

I remember my first kitchen. At its heart was a second-hand, white enamel domestic cooker with one non-working burner. It remained that way when we left. My one cookery book was the now famous *Masterpieces of French Cuisine*. I still have the book. It is much used and battered. The décor was inspired by a one-star Michelin restaurant in Honfleur in Normandy.

From day one I took a tough stand. I had principles, a short fuse, and many times when contemplating an empty restaurant, I would turn people away who had come in without a booking. The writer, Robert Lacey, who was then editor of the *Sunday Times* magazine, was one of those. I did not give him a table and he could not understand why. He hated me for many years. Much later, we became friends.

In Dulwich I experienced every emotion from elation to satisfaction, despair, anger and also quiet anticipation. I knew that I was doing the right thing. I was convinced, and I was excited. I thought I could go a long way. I felt it in my bones. First, we used to commute from a tiny little house in Knightsbridge near the children's school, which was the French Lycée. Eventually, we bought a wonderful Georgian house in Camberwell Grove. We also acquired our lucky dog, a then small, white mongrel named Cassy,

STARTERS

ARTICHOKE AND ASPARAGUS 'MIMOSA'

page 45

SOUFFLÉ OF ROQUEFORT CHEESE WITH PEARS

page 51

SALAD OF CRISPY GUINEA-FOWL

page 58

TERRINE OF FOIE GRAS AND ARTICHOKE

page 59

TERRINE OF CONFIED GUINEA-FOWL

INGREDIENTS

Guinea-fowl legs *8*
Cracked black pepper
Sea salt
Garlic *4 cloves, thinly sliced*
Fresh thyme *½ bunch*
Goose fat *1 litre*
Shallots *8 large, finely chopped*
Butter *50g*
Sherry vinegar *50ml*
Dry sherry *250ml*
Demi-glace *250ml*
Salt and pepper
Cayenne pepper
Ground mace
Ground pimiento

The following recipe, together with the skate on page 102 and the poached guinea-fowl on page 54, is the contribution of my head chef at Simply Nico, Tim Johnson. After spending two and a half years at Chez Nico, he went to France for over a year and worked mainly in the kitchen of Roger Vergé. On his return, he decided that simpler food was more his style. In my opinion, Simply Nico now provides some of the best food anywhere in London.

METHOD/PREPARATION

1. Dry-marinate the guinea-fowl legs with the pepper, salt, garlic and a quarter of the thyme for 24 hours.
2. Rinse the legs under cold running water and pat dry.
3. Melt the goose fat in a large flameproof casserole or ovenproof pan and cook the legs in the fat in an oven pre-heated to 180°C/350°F/gas mark 4 for 1½ hours or until the meat is tender and falls away from the bone. Remove from the oven and leave to cool in the fat.
4. When cool, remove the meat from the bone, discard the skin and flake the flesh.
5. Mix the flaked guinea-fowl with 120ml of the goose fat. Strain the remaining fat and chill in the refrigerator until set.
6. Cook the shallots in the butter until transparent, add the remaining thyme and deglaze the pan with the vinegar.
7. Add the sherry and reduce by half.
8. Add the demi-glace.
9. When you have achieved a nice sauce consistency, mix in the flaked guinea-fowl.
10. Remove the goose fat from the refrigerator and turn out. Remove the jelly from the underside and melt it.

11. Incorporate the melted jelly with the guinea-fowl mixture and season with salt, pepper, cayenne, mace and pimiento.
12. Place in a 1 litre terrine and chill in the refrigerator for 24 hours until set.

PRESENTATION

We serve each slice of this terrine slightly warm with a french bean, shallot and potato salad dressed in balsamic vinegar, oil and a few drizzles of demi-glace.

ROSETTE OF CARAMELIZED SCALLOPS

page 67

SCALLOPS

Scallops are universally popular, but since the demise of so many wet-fishmongers, you hardly ever come across them fresh in shops, though you can get them frozen. This rare harvest from the sea is the nearest one can safely call a restaurant delicacy. In better restaurants they come directly from Scotland, where they are fished from great depths by divers. One of the tricks of the trade is to place the scallops in iced water to make them swell and firm up the flesh.

There is some debate as to whether the roe or coral should be used. Since this part of the scallop is both the reproductive and digestive part of the fish, I never use it. It has a very intense, fishy flavour and the cooking time differs considerably from the flesh. If you cook the coral properly, the scallop will be overcooked. And for me, eating raw coral is unpleasant. In the USA, the law requires that as soon as the scallops are fished, the coral is to be automatically discarded into the sea.

Three ingredients marry well with scallops, and complement each other ideally. First and foremost garlic, then leeks, then mushrooms. Scallops contain a lot of sugar and therefore caramelize well. This recipe, which is one of the most delicious ways to eat scallops, makes the presentation more attractive and unusual to the eye, and by increasing the caramelized area you add intensity of flavour to the sweetness of the dish.

ROSETTE OF CARAMELIZED SCALLOPS

INGREDIENTS

Scallops *8 large, fresh in the shell*
Button mushrooms *16 medium, sliced*
Salt and pepper
Butter and oil *for frying*
Lemon *juice of ½*
Fish velouté *400ml (see page 184)*
Baby spinach leaves *40, tossed in vinaigrette (see page 140)*
Fresh chives *1 small bunch, chopped*
Red pepper coulis *2 tablespoons (see page 168)*

METHOD/PREPARATION

1. Remove the coral and hard membrane from the scallops. Then slice each scallop into 5 escalopes.
2. Place 4 x 12.5 cm pastry rings on squares of kitchen foil or buttered greaseproof paper. Overlap the slices of scallop neatly inside the rings, finishing with one in the centre. Set aside.
3. Season the mushrooms with salt and pepper and fry in a little butter for 2–3 minutes. Place on kitchen paper to absorb the excess fat.
4. Fry the scallop rosettes in a hot, oiled pan until the edges of the scallops caramelize. Season and add the lemon juice. Turn them over with the help of a fish slice and finish cooking.
5. Bring the fish velouté to the boil and reduce to a pouring consistency.

PRESENTATION

1. Arrange 10 spinach leaves in the centre of each plate.
2. Pile equal amounts of mushrooms in the middle of each.
3. Lift the rosette with a fish slice and place on top of the mushrooms. Remove the ring.
4. Spoon the reduced fish velouté over the scallops and garnish with the chives.
5. Decorate with a few drops of red pepper coulis.

CRISPY SALMON WITH SPICY ORIENTAL SAUCE

INGREDIENTS
Salmon escalopes *2 x 180g*
Pickled ginger *25g, sliced*
White cabbage *medium, ½*
Salt *30g*
Sesame oil *150ml*
Icing sugar *50g*
White wine vinegar *100ml*
Sweet sherry *50ml*
Fresh root ginger *20g, finely diced*
Red chilli pepper *1, sliced*
Golden sultanas *100g*
Salt and pepper
Oil *a little, for frying*
Spicy oriental sauce *300ml* *(see page 174)*

This is a one-off recipe, contributed by Martin Hadden, now head chef at the Halcyon Hotel. The only time I really like to eat Chinese food, or Japanese food for that matter, is in a Chinese or Japanese restaurant. I put this dish on my menu as an experiment and before long it was by far the most popular first course. At times the dining-room at Chez Nico at Ninety Park Lane smelt overwhelmingly of oriental cooking and I felt extremely uneasy. After two years, I decided to take it off the menu because I prefer the smell of truffle oil and truffles to that of sesame oil.

METHOD/PREPARATION
1. Cut each salmon escalope into 4 even squares.
2. Cut each square into 6 even slices, retaining the original shape.
3. Thread 6 slices on to each of 4 kebab skewers, alternating the slices with thick pieces of pickled ginger. Set aside.
4. Break the cabbage into individual leaves, remove any thick stems and shred the leaves very finely.
5. Sprinkle the cabbage with the salt, cover and leave in the refrigerator for 4–6 hours. Then wash thoroughly to remove the salt and drain well.
6. Heat the sesame oil in a large saucepan and add the cabbage. Stir well for about 30 seconds. Push the cabbage to one side, add the sugar and cook until it starts to caramelize. Stir back the cabbage and mix.
7. Add the vinegar, sherry, fresh ginger, chilli and sultanas and cook over a high heat for 2–3 minutes or until all the liquid has evaporated. The cabbage should be light golden in colour and slightly crispy. Allow to cool before adjusting the seasoning.

8. Season the salmon with salt and pepper and cook skin side down in a flat frying pan lightly coated in oil, until golden and crisp. Turn and finish cooking to taste, preferably leaving the centre a little underdone.
9. Reheat the cabbage.

PRESENTATION

1. Place a small mound of cabbage in the centre of each plate.
2. Place the salmon on top.
3. Spoon the sauce around.

ASSIETTE GOURMANDE OF SMOKED SALMON AND CAVIAR

page 71

RAVIOLI OF LOBSTER WITH TRUFFLE SAUCE

page 74

BLINIS

INGREDIENTS

Wholewheat flour *175g*
Sugar *1 tablespoon*
Salt *1 teaspoon*
Butter *100g, softened*
Egg yolks *2*
Milk *110ml*
Fresh yeast *5g*
Egg whites
Oil *a little, for frying*

These are small pancakes, traditional in Russia, that we serve with caviar and soured cream. You can prepare the basic mix and keep it in the refrigerator for about 5–6 days. Then take approximately 1 tablespoon of the dough to make batches of 14–15.

METHOD/PREPARATION

1. Mix the flour, sugar and salt in a large bowl.
2. Rub the butter into the flour mixture.
3. Add the egg yolks.
4. Warm the milk and dissolve the yeast in it.
5. Stir the yeast liquid into the flour mixture. (At this stage you can store it in the refrigerator.)
6. Take a heaped tablespoon of the batter, place in a bowl, cover with clingfilm and keep in a warm place until double in size.
7. Whisk the egg whites to smooth, soft peaks and fold gently into the risen batter. Allow 3 egg whites per rounded tablespoon of mixture.
8. If you have 5–7.5cm round galette moulds, brush them lightly with a little oil, half-fill them with the batter, place them on a hot griddle and cook until golden on both sides. Or, in a large, non-stick, lightly oiled frying pan, spoon out small dollops of the mixture which you can flatten and shape with a spatula, cooking on both sides until golden.

LANGOUSTINE SOUP

INGREDIENTS

Fresh langoustine shells *1 kg*
Oil *a little*
Brandy *300 ml*
Tomato purée *200g*
Dry white wine *500 ml*
Butter *100g*
Carrots *8, chopped*
Onions *2, thinly sliced*
Fennel *2 bulbs, chopped*
Garlic *1 clove, finely chopped*
Plum tomatoes *1 x 500g can*
Fresh tomatoes *500g*
Fresh thyme *1 small bunch*
Bay leaf *1*
Star anise *1*
Black peppercorns *10*
Salt
Fish stock *1.2 litres (see page 247)*
Water *1.2 litres*
Double cream *1 litre*
Lemon juice *a squeeze*

I think the taste of langoustine is far superior to that of lobster. Its flesh is sweet and the flavour its shell imparts is unmistakable. This soup, which is the first course on our gastronomic menu, is rich and quite delicious. We finish it off with a little truffle-flavoured sabayon.

METHOD/PREPARATION

1. In the oven preheated to 230°C/450°F/gas mark 8 roast the langoustine shells in a little oil in a roasting pan until golden, then deglaze the pan with the brandy and tomato purée.
2. Cook for about 10 minutes, then add the wine and reduce the liquid by half. Keep on one side until the vegetables are ready.
3. In a large saucepan, melt the butter and sauté the carrots, onions, fennel and garlic until lightly coloured. Add the canned and fresh tomatoes, the herbs and star anise, peppercorns and salt.
4. Crush the langoustine shells and add them and their reduced cooking liquid to the vegetable mixture.
5. Cover with the stock and water and bring to the boil. Remove any scum that may rise to the surface. Then leave to simmer for 1½ hours.
6. Strain through a fine sieve and reduce to about 250 ml.
7. Add the cream, adjust the seasoning and add the lemon juice.
8. Just before serving, we add a coffee spoon of truffle sabayon to each serving. This is a mixture of hollandaise sauce and whipped cream with a few drops of truffle essence. Then each serving is flashed under a hot grill and glazed.

CONSOMMÉ OF MUSHROOM WITH MADEIRA

INGREDIENTS
Button mushrooms *450g*
Fresh foie gras *40g*
Onion *100g, very finely chopped*
Tomato purée *1 heaped tablespoon*
Chicken stock *2 litres* *(see page 245)*
Madeira *6 tablespoons*
Salt
Egg whites *5*
Fresh coriander leaves

In a lifetime of cooking there are only a handful of dishes that one can possibly claim as one's own. When this consommé is well made, the colour and sparkle of the soup against a shiny silver spoon is stunning. I am very proud of this particular dish which somehow has stuck fast to my name.

METHOD/PREPARATION
1. Mince the mushrooms in a food processor.
2. Melt the foie gras in a large saucepan, add the onion and sauté until transparent.
3. Add the tomato purée, stock and mushrooms, madeira and salt and cook for about 1 hour.
4. Pass through a fine sieve and allow to cool.
5. Whisk the egg whites to soft peaks and slowly add the liquid to them, beating continuously until well amalgamated.
6. Place the soup over a very low heat and simmer for about 35 minutes to clarify the liquid, then pass through 2–3 layers of muslin.
7. Serve in bowls with fresh coriander leaves floating on top.

FISH

ESCALOPE OF SALMON WITH POACHED EGG AND FISH VELOUTÉ RISOTTO

page 88

FRESHWATER PERCH WITH CRISPY PASTA

page 93

GRILLED JOHN DORY WITH ROSEMARY BEURRE BLANC

INGREDIENTS
John Dory *4 fillets, cut in half*
Salt and pepper
Plain flour *a dusting*
Oil *a little*
Lemon juice *a squeeze*
Spinach *400g cooked*
(see page 140)
Butter *1 tablespoon*
Potato purée *200g*
(see page 156)
Button onions *12, glazed*
(see page 153)
Beurre blanc *300ml*
(see page 181)
Fresh rosemary *1 sprig*
Fresh chervil *12 sprigs*

If you get a large fish of 1.25kg you should be able to get 4 decent-sized fillets from it. Each portion is cut in half in the shape of a diamond.

METHOD/PREPARATION
1. Season the John Dory fillets with salt and pepper and dust them with flour. Brush lightly with oil.
2. Cook them on a hot griddle, skin side down, until golden and crispy. Turn them over and finish cooking.
3. Remove from the griddle and drain on kitchen paper. Sprinkle with lemon juice.
4. Warm the spinach with the butter and then season.
5. Warm the potato purée.
6. Warm the onions.
7. Heat the beurre blanc and infuse with the sprig of rosemary. Do not boil.

PRESENTATION
1. In a bowl or plate, arrange 3 piles of spinach equidistant one from the other, with a glazed onion on top.
2. Make a little bed of potato purée.
3. Place the divided John Dory fillets on top of the purée, slightly over-lapping.
4. Spoon the rosemary beurre blanc all around and garnish with 3 of the chervil sprigs.

RED MULLET WITH BASIL PURÉE

INGREDIENTS

Red mullet *4 x 150g fillets*
Salt and pepper
Plain flour *a dusting*
Oil *a little, for frying*
Red wine *1 litre*
Demi-glace *300ml*
(see page 248)
Garlic *1 clove*
Fresh rosemary *1 sprig*
Butter
Lemon *juice of ¼*
Basil purée quenelles
4 rounded tablespoons
(see page 147)

METHOD/PREPARATION

1. Make a couple of incisions on the skin side of the fish. Season with salt and pepper and dust lightly with flour.
2. Fry the mullet fillets in a little oil until the skin is golden and crispy. Turn them over and finish cooking.
3. In a saucepan reduce the wine by one-third, add the demi-glace and reduce to a nice syrupy consistency.
4. Infuse with the garlic and rosemary for 10–15 minutes, then pass through a sieve.
5. Finish the sauce by whisking in a few small knobs of butter.
6. Squeeze a little lemon juice over the red mullet.

PRESENTATION

1. Place a large warmed quenelle of basil purée in the centre of each large bowl.
2. Pour the sauce around the basil purée.
3. Place the red mullet fillet on top of the quenelle.

NUGGETS OF FRESH SALMON WITH LANGOUSTINE

page 103

CN

MEAT

SHIN OF VEAL BRAISED IN MADEIRA

page 111

BOUDIN BLANC WITH SPINACH AND APPLE SAUCE

page 120

'RAGOÛT' OF CHICKEN WITH WILD MUSHROOMS

page 124

CN

BREAST OF DUCK WITH CRUSHED PEPPERCORNS AND HONEY

page 128

BREAST OF DUCK WITH CRUSHED PEPPERCORNS AND HONEY

INGREDIENTS
Duck breasts *4 x 80g*
Salt and pepper
Oil *a little, for frying*
Dark honey *4 tablespoons*
Black peppercorns *4 teaspoons crushed*
Pakchoi *4*
Butter *a knob*
Cassis sauce *300ml* *(see page 175)*
Blackcurrants *24, fresh or frozen*
Sarladaise potatoes *4* *(see page 158)*
Shallots *12, caramelized*
Fresh chervil *4 sprigs*

METHOD/PREPARATION
1. Season the duck breasts with salt and pepper.
2. Brush the frying pan with a little oil, put in the breasts skin side down and cook slowly over a medium heat for about 8–10 minutes. This will first of all render the fat and then crispen the skin.
3. Turn over and cook for about 30 seconds.
4. At the same time, brush the skin side with honey and sprinkle with the peppercorns.
5. Turn over again to seal and caramelize, then allow to rest for 5 minutes. Cut each breast into 6 even pieces.
6. Boil the pakchoi in salted water until tender. Toss in butter and season.
7. Warm the sauce and blackcurrants.
8. Have the sarladaise potatoes and shallots ready.

PRESENTATION
1. Place the potatoes in the centre of each plate, then place the pakchoi on top, followed by the shallots.
2. Surround with the pieces of duck.
3. Spoon the sauce and blackcurrants evenly around.
4. Garnish the shallots with the chervil.

CONFIT OF DUCK

INGREDIENTS

Duck legs *4*
Rock salt *1 tablespoon*
Black peppercorns *1 tablespoon crushed*
Garlic *1 clove, thinly sliced*
Fresh thyme *4 sprigs*
Bay leaves *2, crushed*
Duck fat *2 litres*

This dish is now being served up and down the country. I first served it in Battersea in 1981, and remember well that I had some trouble finding the goose fat which we used at the time. I am pleased that I contributed so much towards popularizing this dish, because I think it makes an ideal meal and is a great way of using up duck legs, which can be quite tough.

In our version of how to 'confit' duck legs we serve the confit with sarladaise potatoes, boiled pakchoi and spicy oriental sauce. You can also serve it with salad, or a light madeira sauce. In fact, it is a very versatile dish. What is more, you can cook the duck legs in advance and keep them stored for up to 2 weeks if kept in duck fat in the fridge.

METHOD/PREPARATION

1. Cover the duck legs with all the spices, garlic and herbs and dry-marinate for 24 hours.
2. Rinse the legs under cold running water to remove all evidence of the spices.
3. Melt the duck fat in a large pan, add the duck legs and simmer very gently for about 2½ hours.
4. Leave the legs to cool and store in the fat.
5. When needed, take a little of the duck fat and melt it in a frying pan. Then sauté the legs, skin side down, until golden and crispy.

PIGEON WITH BOUDIN AND REDCURRANTS

INGREDIENTS

Oven-ready pigeons *4 x 500g*
Salt and pepper
Oil *a little, for frying*
Clear honey *100ml*
Boudin blanc *1 (see page 120)*
Potato purée *300g (see page 156)*
Cream of garlic *50g (see page 152)*
Port *200ml*
Demi-glace *300ml (see page 248)*
Fresh thyme *1 sprig*
Garlic *1 clove*
Redcurrants *about 40, fresh or frozen*
Roast garlic *4 cloves (see page 152)*
Apple *8 discs, poached*

METHOD/PREPARATION

1. Season the pigeons with salt and pepper and fry them in some of the oil until evenly coloured on all sides.
2. Place them in the oven preheated to 230°C/450°F/gas mark 8 for about 8 minutes, basting frequently. Paint them with honey and cook for a further 2 minutes. Then remove them from the oven and leave to rest for about 10 minutes. Reserve the juices from the roasting pan.
3. Remove the skin from the boudin and slice into 8 even pieces, then fry until golden on both sides.
4. Remove the legs from the pigeons and finish cooking by frying gently.
5. Return the breasts to the oven for a couple of minutes to warm and pour in the reserved roasting juices.
6. Mix the potato purée and the cream of garlic and heat through.
7. For the sauce, reduce the port by three-quarters. Then add the demi-glace, thyme and garlic. Reduce further, until you get a glossy consistency, then pass through a sieve. Add three-quarters of the redcurrants to the sauce and warm it.

PRESENTATION

1. Place the potato purée in the centre of each plate.
2. Remove the pigeon breasts from the bone and place 2 on top of the purée with a leg to each side.
3. Garnish with 2 slices of boudin, a roast garlic clove, and 2 discs of apple.
4. Spoon the sauce around and sprinkle with about 10 redcurrants.

PIGEON WITH BOUDIN AND REDCURRANTS

page 131

VEGETABLES

VEGETABLES AND GARNISHES

BRAISED SAVOY CABBAGE

INGREDIENTS

Butter *a knob*
Shallots *2 large, sliced*
Savoy cabbage *1 medium, chopped*
Chicken stock *(see page 245)*
Salt and pepper
Chestnuts *150g, whole, poached*

METHOD/PREPARATION

1. Melt some of the butter in a pan and sweat the shallots.
2. Add the cabbage.
3. Cover with chicken stock and braise slowly until cooked. Season to taste with salt and pepper and add the chestnuts and the remaining butter.

BRAISED FENNEL

INGREDIENTS

Fennel *4 bulbs*
Onion *1 small, thinly sliced*
Garlic *3 cloves, crushed*
Olive oil *100ml*
Fresh thyme *1 sprig*
Fresh rosemary *1 sprig*
Lemon *1, juice of*
Salt and pepper

METHOD/PREPARATION

1. Clean, trim and cut the fennel bulbs in half.
2. In a flameproof dish or pan sweat the onion and garlic in the oil.
3. Add the herbs, lemon juice and salt and pepper.
4. Add the fennel.
5. Pour enough water into the pan to cover the fennel.
6. Cover the pan with a paper cartouche (a circle of greaseproof paper cut the same diameter as the pan, with a small hole in the middle to let the steam escape).
7. Bring to the boil, then cook in the oven preheated to 180°C/350°F/gas mark 4 for about 35–45 minutes until tender.
8. Remove from the oven and leave to cool in the bouillon.
9. When cold, store the fennel, steeped in the strained bouillon in a glass jar, in the refrigerator.

SPINACH AND FRENCH BEANS

Both spinach and French beans are excellent cooked with no embellishment. I am not one of those who believe that spinach should be dry-cooked in a pan with butter. I prefer to blanch it in large quantities of boiling salted water, then drain and squeeze it. After this it should be very carefully cooked in lots of butter over a very slow heat and allowed to absorb the butter so that it becomes unctuous and soft. Lemon should never be squeezed over spinach because it goes brown quickly. The only flavours one should add are small quantities of garlic, a little salt, pepper and nutmeg. If water keeps oozing out of the spinach while it is cooked, it should be drained well. Before serving, tip on to some kitchen paper. This way it hardly needs either meat or fish to accompany it but becomes a meal in itself.

The first rule to remember when cooking French beans is never to cook them in large quantities. There isn't a flame strong enough, even on a catering stove, to boil water sufficiently fiercely. Beans must cook before they start to lose their colour and the only way to do this is when the ratio of the beans to water is very low. The second rule is that you must cool them down as fast as possible. You therefore need to have ready ice-cold water, preferably water with lots of ice cubes floating in it. And the only way to enjoy their full flavour is to cook beans to a point just before they are ready to come apart. Don't make the mistake of leaving beans *al dente*. That way you lose fifty per cent of the taste. I also prefer not to top and tail the beans with a knife, but to snap the ends off by hand. Butter, garlic, salt and pepper and/or very, very finely chopped shallots can be used to flavour them. Served cold with the right dressing, they make a delicious salad.

CELERIAC PURÉE

INGREDIENTS
Celeriac *1kg*
Butter *100g*
Salt and pepper
Double cream *100ml*

METHOD/PREPARATION
1. Wash and peel the celeriac.
2. Cut it into 2.5cm cubes.
3. Melt the butter in a heavy saucepan, add the cubes of celeriac, season with salt and pepper, cover the pan with a lid and cook very slowly until tender but not coloured. Stir occasionally so that the celeriac does not stick.
4. Add the cream and reduce by half.
5. Liquidize the contents of the pan to a purée.
6. Check the seasoning and pass through a fine sieve.

CANNELLONI OF VEGETABLES

INGREDIENTS
Carrots *2*
Red pepper *1*
Leek *1*
Courgettes *2*
Celeriac *1, small*
Butter *50g*
Salt and pepper
Fresh pasta *4 x 10cm squares* *(see page 250)*

You can use any mixture of vegetables and flavour them with various herbs and spices.

As well as an accompaniment to a meat dish, this can be served as a vegetarian starter.

METHOD/PREPARATION
1. Wash and peel all the vegetables and cut into julienne (fine strips).
2. Blanch them in boiling salted water, then plunge them into ice-cold water.
3. Drain the vegetables well, and dry on kitchen paper.
4. Sauté them lightly in the butter and season with salt and pepper.
5. Stuff each pasta square with a quarter of the vegetable mixture and roll into a cannelloni shape.
6. Wrap in clingfilm.
7. To reheat, place in a steamer for 5–6 minutes.
8. To serve, trim both ends and remove the clingfilm.

VEGETABLE GARNISH

INGREDIENTS
Potatoes *4 medium*
Clarified butter *50g*
Onions *2, sliced*
Caster sugar *a pinch*
Fresh thyme *a pinch of fresh or dried*
Courgettes *2*
Aubergine *1*
Olive oil
Salt and pepper
Butter *a little*
Spinach leaves *900g, cooked (see page 140)*
Garlic *8 cloves, roasted (see page 152)*

In the restaurant, we serve this with Saddle of Lamb with a Herb Crust and Couscous (see page 115).

METHOD/PREPARATION
1. Peel the potatoes and trim both ends.
2. Pare the potatoes into a tube shape 5cm in diameter, then slice very thinly with a knife or mandolin.
3. Fry the potatoes in a pan in some of the butter until cooked and golden but firm.
4. Caramelize the onions in a little butter with the sugar and thyme.
5. Cut the courgettes at a slight angle into slices 5mm thick.
6. Cut the aubergine in half lengthways, then cut into slices 5mm thick.
7. Pan-fry the aubergine and courgettes in oil until golden on both sides and season with salt and pepper. Absorb the excess oil with kitchen paper.
8. Layer the aubergine and courgettes alternately (3 layers of each) in 4 x 10cm diameter moulds and keep warm.
9. In 4 moulds (the same as those for the aubergine and courgettes) arrange the slices of potato, starting in the centre, to form a full circle. Cover the potato with a thin layer of caramelized onion. Repeat these layerings.
10. Place the four potato garnishes on a griddle over a medium heat, adding a little fresh butter and turning the potatoes until golden on both sides.

PRESENTATION
1. Unmould the vegetables and place in the centre of each plate. Put the unmoulded potatoes on top.
2. Put 2 small piles of spinach on each side of the plate with 1 piece of warmed, roast garlic on top of each.

STUFFED COURGETTES AND TOMATOES

Courgettes and tomatoes are ideal vegetables to stuff and perfect to accompany lamb. Courgettes need to be blanched and cooked really well before stuffing. Before presenting them, paint them with heavily scented and well-seasoned clarified butter. You can also crenellate the sides to make them more attractive.

With tomatoes you can either remove the skin by making a little incision, dropping them in hot water and then quickly peeling the skin off. Or quarter them and remove the seeds, then run the point of a very sharp knife between the skin and the flesh.

The stuffing is interchangeable; ratatouille, basil purée, rice, minced meat, or simply tomato concassé flavoured with Provençal herbs, garlic and parsley.

TURBOT WITH CRISPY POTATO AND CEP PURÉE

page 98

SEA BASS WITH OLIVE CRUST AND BASIL PURÉE

page 92

MILK-FED VEAL CUTLET WITH GIROLLES AND POTATO GALETTE

page 110

SADDLE OF LAMB WITH A HERB CRUST AND COUSCOUS

page 115

SAUCES

RAVIOLI OF GOAT'S CHEESE WITH RED PEPPER COULIS

page 49

CRISPY SALMON WITH SPICY ORIENTAL SAUCE

page 68

GRILLED JOHN DORY WITH ROSEMARY BEURRE BLANC

page 96

PUDDINGS

PUDDINGS, SAUCES AND SYRUPS

SORBETS AND ICE CREAMS

I firmly believe that a well-balanced 3-course meal should be composed of either a cold or a *tiède* starter, a hot main course and a cold pudding, preferably a mixture of fresh fruit and sorbets, or fresh fruit and ice cream. My favourite ice creams are vanilla, pistachio and caramel. My favourite sorbets are passion fruit, cassis and, when it is perfect, pear. How good the sorbet finally is depends entirely on the quality and ripeness – in fact it should be slightly over-ripe – of the fruit of your choice. The possibilities are numerous, from wild strawberries and melon, to pineapple and pink grapefruit. The best sorbet I ever served was in Battersea and was made of lychees. I prefer the classic recipes and have never made tea, sage or lavender-flavoured sorbets, nor indeed rosemary and thyme ones. The most unforgettable sorbet I ever had was Paul Bocuse's raspberry one. I also intensely dislike frozen yoghurt because it is neither one thing nor the other.

The basic recipe is very similar. I usually tend to reduce sugar syrup to lose quite a lot of water when there is a very high acid content in the fruit such as grapefruit. This way you get a much softer sorbet. The length of time the sorbet or ice cream is left in the machine varies for each one. To the professional chef, the texture required is registered in the eye. In my opinion, it is not worth attempting to make either a sorbet or an ice cream unless you have an ice-cream machine.

CHOCOLATE SORBET

INGREDIENTS

Extra-bitter chocolate *150g*
(minimum 70% cocoa solids)
Cocoa powder *75g*
Caster sugar *250g*
Water *500ml*

METHOD/PREPARATION

1. Chop the chocolate into very small pieces and add the cocoa powder.
2. Make a sugar syrup by combining the water and sugar in a saucepan, bringing it to the boil and simmering it for fifteen minutes.
3. Whisk the syrup into the chocolate.
4. When it has all melted and the mixture is smooth, leave to cool.
5. Turn in an ice-cream machine.

SORBETS AND FRESH FRUITS WITH LIME SYRUP

TULIP OF FRESH FRUIT AND VANILLA ICE CREAM

page 195

WARM CHOCOLATE MOUSSE WITH PISTACHIO ICE CREAM

page 205

BURNT LEMON CREAM WITH RASPBERRIES

page 208

LEMON TART WITH CASSIS SAUCE

page 213

CHOCOLATE TART WITH ORANGE FLAVOURED CUSTARD

page 216

PETITS FOURS

PETITS FOURS

GRAND PLATE OF ASSORTED MINI DESSERTS

BASICS

SAVOURY PASTRY

INGREDIENTS

Plain flour *500g*
Butter *250g, diced*
Salt *a pinch*
Egg *1*
Iced water *190ml*

METHOD/PREPARATION

1. To obtain the best results place all the ingredients including the food processor bowl into the freezer for about 30 minutes before use.
2. Place the flour, butter and salt in the food processor and mix at high speed until the mixture becomes smooth.
3. Add the egg and pour the iced water over slowly while mixing.
4. Remove the dough and knead gently by hand.
5. Wrap the pastry in clingfilm and rest in the refrigerator for at least 1 hour, or until needed.

BASIC PASTA DOUGH

INGREDIENTS

Flour *1kg*
Salt *a good pinch*
Eggs *4 made up to 400ml with saffron water (water infused with a few strands of saffron, then strained)*

METHOD/PREPARATION

1. Sieve the flour into a food processor bowl. Add the salt.
2. Switch on to medium speed and slowly pour in the saffron-and-egg mixture.
3. When the mixture comes together as a dough, place it on a clean work surface and knead for 5–10 minutes until smooth.
4. Leave to rest for 1 hour.
5. To get the best possible result, the dough must be rolled several times through a pasta machine, folding each time.
6. Once it is rolled out to the correct thickness and consistency it can be used as it is for ravioli, or cannelloni. If you want to make spaghetti or other types of pasta you need the required cutter attachments.

RECIPE INDEX

References to illustrations are in *italic*.

Rice,
Basmati Rice, 163
Risotto, 80
Cep Risotto, 80
Escalope of Salmon with Poached Egg and Fish Velouté Risotto, 88, *90–91*
Roast Garlic, 152
Roquefort,
Soufflé of Roquefort Cheese with Pears, 51, *52–3*

Sablé Pastry, 209
Saffron,
Mussel Soup with Saffron, 81
Salads,
Salad of Crispy Guinea-Fowl, *56–7*, 58
Salad of Poached Guinea-Fowl with Fresh Figs, 54–5
salads and vinaigrettes, 180
Salmon,
Assiette Gourmande of Smoked Salmon and Caviar, 71, *72–3*
Crispy Salmon with Spicy Oriental Sauce, 68–9, *176–7*
Escalopes of Salmon with Crispy Lettuce, Spring Onions and Coriander, 104–5
Escalope of Salmon with Poached Egg and Fish Velouté Risotto, 88, *90–91*
Marinated Salmon, 74
Nuggets of Fresh Salmon with Langoustine, *100–101*, 103
Paupiettes of Salmon, 70
Salmon and Scallop Mousse Stuffing for Lobster Ravioli, 75
Sauces (savoury),
general, 167
Apple Sauce, 168
'Barigoule' Sauce, 186
Béarnaise Sauce, 178
Béchamel, 187
Beurre Blanc, 181
Cassis Sauce, 175
Cep Sauce, 169
Fish Velouté, 184
Gazpacho, 185
Hollandaise, 178
Mayonnaise, 179
Madeira, 184
Mustard Sauce, 175
Onion Sauce, 172
Red Pepper Coulis, 168
Sauce for Chicken, 186
Sauce for Guinea-Fowl Salad, 185
Spicy Oriental Sauce, 174
Tartare Sauce, 179
Tomato and Basil Sauce, 173
Truffle Sauce, 172
Sauces and Syrups (sweet),
Apricot Sauce, 219
Caramel Sauce, 219
Cassis Sauce, 212
Chocolate Sauce, 219
Lime Syrup, 217
Raspberry Coulis, 218
Sugar Syrup, 217
Savoury Pastry, 250
Scallops, 66
Rosette of Caramelized Scallops, *64–5*, 67
Salmon and Scallop Mousse Stuffing for Lobster Ravioli, 75
Sea Bass with Olive Crust and Basil Purée, 92, *148–9*
Shallots,
Sweet Shallots, 156
Skate,
Roast Wings of Skate with a Green Peppercorn Crust and 'Barigoule' Sauce, 102
Solettes with Cep Sauce, 89
Sorbets, *see* Puddings
Soufflés, 50
Coffee and Rum Soufflé, 204
Soufflé of Roquefort Cheese with Pears, 51, 52–3
Soups,
Consommé of Mushroom with Madeira, 83
Langoustine Soup, 82
Mussel Soup with Saffron, 81
Spinach, 140
Starters, 43
Artichoke and Asparagus 'Mimosa', 45, *46–47*
Assiette Gourmande of Smoked Salmon and Caviar, 71, *72–3*
Blinis, 78, *79*
Cep Risotto, 80
Consommé of Mushroom with Madeira, 83
Crispy Salmon with Spicy Oriental Sauce, *68–9*
Langoustine Soup, 82
Marinated Salmon, 74
Mussel Soup with Saffron, 81
Paupiettes of Salmon, 70
Ravioli of Goat's Cheese, 45
Ravioli of Lobster with Truffle Sauce, 74–5, *76–7*
Rosette of Caramelized Scallops, *64–5*, 67
Salad of Poached Guinea-Fowl with Fresh Figs, 54–5
Salmon and Scallop Mousse Stuffing for Lobster Ravioli, 75
Soufflé of Roquefort Cheese with Pears, 51, *52–3*
Terrine of Confied Guinea-Fowl, 62–3
Terrine of Foie Gras and Artichoke, 59, *60–61*
Stocks,
Brown Chicken Stock, 246
Demi-Glace, 116, 134, 248, 250
Fish Stock, 247
Vegetable Stock, 249
White Chicken Stock, 245
Sugar Syrup, 217
Sweet Shallots, 156
Sweetbreads with Parma Ham and Morels, 117
Sweetcorn,
Sweetcorn Pancakes, 151
Tartare Sauce, 179
Tarts,
Apple Tart, 212
Chocolate Tart, 214–15, 216
Lemon Tart with Cassis Sauce, 210–11, 213
Terrines,
Terrine of Confied Guinea-Fowl, 62–3
Terrine of Foie Gras and Artichoke, 59, *60–61*
Tomatoes,
Stuffed Courgettes and Tomatoes, 143
Tomato and Basil Sauce, 173
Truffle Sauce, 172
Tuiles, 230
Tulip of Fresh Fruit and Vanilla Ice Cream, 195, *196–7*
Turbot with Crispy Potato and Cep Purée, 98, *144–5*

Vanilla Ice Cream, 195
Veal,
Milk-Fed Veal Cutlets with Girolles and Potato Galette, 110, *154–5*
Shin of Veal Braised in Madeira, 111, *112–13*
Veal Kidneys with Bay Leaves, 116
Vegetables,
Cannelloni of Vegetables, 141
Celeriac Purée, 141
Cream of Garlic, 152
French beans, 140
Glazed Onions, 153
lentils, 159
potatoes, *see* potatoes
Roast Garlic, 152
spinach, 140
Stuffed Courgettes and Tomatoes, 143
Sweet Shallots, 146, 156
Sweetcorn Pancakes, 151
Vegetable Garnish, 115, 142
vegetable stock, 249
see also Mushrooms

White Chicken Stock, 245

GENERAL INDEX

References to illustrations are in *italic*.

Academy of Gastronomes, 167
Ainsworth, Jim, 32

Barry, Michael, 33
Battersea, London, 18–21
Binns, Richard, 20
Blanc, Raymond, 31
Box Tree Restaurant, Ilkley, 31
British cuisine and palate, 28–32
  New British Cuisine, 32
Brown, Derek, 24, 26
Bulmer, Derek, 24
Burton-Race, John, 20
Business Expansion Schemes (BES), 20

Callas, Provence, 15, 23–4
Carrier, Robert, 31
Caterer and Hotelkeeper, 21, 33
Chef Patron concept, 23
Chez Nico at Ninety Park Lane, 14, 22–3, *25*, 29
  family staff members, 14
Chez Nico Battersea, 18–20, 24
Chez Nico Dulwich, 13, 17–18, 31–2, 35
Chez Nico Shinfield, 13, 20–21, 32
cookery books, 31
La Coupole Restaurant, Paris, 35
Crewe, Quentin, 31
Cuisine du Soleil (Vergé), 18
Cuisine et Vins de France (Curnonsky), 167
Cuisine Gourmande (Guérard), 31
Cuisine Minceur (Guérard), 31
Curnonsky (Maurice Edmond Saillaud), 167
customer relations, 13, 17, 35

David, Elizabeth, 31
Driver, Christopher, 31–2

Egon Ronay Guide, 19, 32
Evening News, 32
Evening Standard, 26, 35
Eysenck, Sybil, 31–2

Fan, Richard, 21
food purchases, 14, 28, 29
Fort, Matthew, 33
Forte, Rocco, 23
French chefs, 31

Garrett, André, 47
Gastronomic Tour of France (Crewe), 31
Gavroche Restaurant, Lower Sloane Street, 31
Giquel, Jean-Luc, 26, 33
Good Food Guide, 13, 19, 31–2, 80
  Pestle and Mortar award, 19, 32
Gourgey, Maurice, 20
Great Chefs of France (Crewe), 18
Great Dishes of the World (Carrier), 31
Guérard, Michel, 31

Hall, Aileen, 32
Hannan, Brian, 33
Harris, Clifford, 21
Hole in the Wall, Bath, 31
Hyam, Joe, 33
Jaine, Tom, 32
Johnson, Tim, 62

kitchen equipment, 38
Koffman, Pierre, 31

Lacey, Robert, 17
Ladenis, Dinah-Jane, 11–12, 14, 15–17, 20, 23–4, 26, 31, 32
Ladenis, Natasha, 11–12, 24
Lanchester, John, 33
Lawrie, Colonel Aitken, 17
Lipton, Gerald, 22, 23

Maschler, Fay, 33, 35
Meades, Jonathan, 21, 33
measurements, 39
Mediterranean food, 28–9
menus, 14, *30*
  choosing dishes, 29–30
  gastronomic, *30*, 36
  ingredients, 28–9
Michelin Guide, 32
  French restaurants, 20, 21, 31
  Nico, 12, 17, 18–19, 23, 24–8
  other English restaurants, 31
Mosimann, Anton, 31
Moulin de Mougins, Cannes, 18
Murkett, Tony, 23
My Gastronomy (Nico Ladenis), 21

Napley, Sir David, 20, 24
Nico Central (restaurant), 13, 23, 27–8

Oasis Restaurant, La Napoule, 22
Outhier, Louis, 22–3

Payton, Bob, 21, 24
Perry-Smith, George, 31
Peskin, Richard, 21
philosophy of cooking, 29
Posh Nosh (TV programme), 18

restaurants,
  designer restaurants, 35
  guides and critics, 31–5
Rhodes, Paul, *29*
Round, Jeremy, 32
Roux, Albert, 31
Roux, Michel, 18, 20, 24, 31

Simply Nico, Rochester Row, London, 20–21
Smith, Drew, 32
Smith, Michael, 18
Sunday Times, 15, 31

Tatler, 33
Time Out, 33
The Times, 21, 33

Vergé, Roger, 18

Waterside Inn, Bray, 24
White, Marco Pierre, 31
Williams, Gareth, 21
Winner, Michael, 11–12, 33

Nico Ladenis